What Sea Creature Is This?

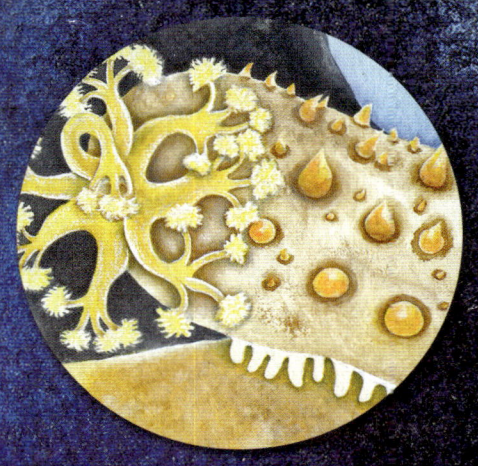

NANCY KELLY ALLEN
Illustrated by GLORIA BROWN

A Red Pebble Book
from Red Rock Press
New York New York

For Evan—N.K.A.

For Natalie and Nadiyah—G.B.

What Sea Creature Is This?

978-1933176-41-3

Text copyright 2012 © Nancy Kelly Allen
Illustrations copyright 2012 © Gloria Brown

Design by Susan Smilanic, Studio 21 Design & Advertising.
Durango, Colorado

Red Rock Press
New York, New York

www.RedRockPress.com

All rights reserved. No part of this book may be reproduced, stored in a retrieval system or transmitted by any means without the written consent of Red Rock Press. Inquiries should be directed to rights@RedRockPress.com.
Library of Congress Cataloging-in-Publication Data

Allen, Nancy Kelly, 1949-
 What sea creature is this? / by Nancy Kelly Allen ; illustrations by Gloria Brown.
     p. cm.
 ISBN 978-1-933176-41-3
 1. Marine animals--Juvenile literature. I. Brown, Gloria, 1953- , ill. II. Title.
 QL122.2.A45 2012
 591.77--dc23
                2011040171

from Red Rock Press

What Sea Creature Is This?

What sea creature is this, working as a toothbrush?

This cleaner-fish is called a Wrasse.

Wrasses operate "cleaning stations," something like underwater car washes, where larger fish come to get rid of the small, annoying crustaceans, called parasites, that cling to their bodies. A wrasse also clears away a client's dead scales.

Wrasses are the only fish that swim into the mouth of a shark and swim out again. As soon as the shark opens its mouth wide, the cleaner fish pick out the food bits stuck between the shark's teeth. You might say that the wrasse is the world's bravest toothbrush.

What sea creature is this, pretty as a flower?

This is a Sea Anemone.

Looking at these underwater lovelies is like looking at a garden blazing in red, pink and aqua blooms. As with real flowers, some sea anemones measure not even an inch while others are six feet in diameter. Don't pick sea flowers! A touch may trigger a poisonous sting by their needle-like tentacles. Clownfish, however, are immune to sea-anemone toxin and swim close by, using sea anemones as bodyguards against other hungry sea creatures.

What sea creature is this, shining a light?

This is a Flashlight Fish.

Many live in deep, dark waters. Under their eyes are pouches filled with bacteria, which make them shine like flashlights. Sometimes the light is white. Other times, the light is blue, yellow or green. And with a blink, the lights go out. Flashlight fish in shallow water are about six inches long. Those in deep ocean water are twice that length.

What sea creature is this, imitating a stone?

This is a Stonefish.

The foot-long stonefish is unnoticeable in its rocky habitat or half-buried in sand. Rock-still, it appears harmless. *Not!* The spiny stonefish is the most poisonous fish in the water. If a shark or stingray bumps into the stonefish, its back spines stick straight up to stab the predator, then spurt poison into the enemy's wounds. But when tasty smaller fish or shrimp swim by, the stonefish opens its wide mouth and whooshes in its meal. *Gulp!* Lunch is swallowed whole.

What sea creature is this, breaking apart?

This is a Sea Cucumber.

Some are short — under an inch long. Others stretch out to about six feet. But even tiny sea cucumbers are tricksters. A sea cucumber can break itself into pieces.

If the sea cucumber is attacked, it squirts out sticky stuff, parts of its insides, to confuse the predator. Then the sea cucumber (or most of it) escapes! Missing parts are no problem for the sea cucumber — it just grows new ones. This is called regeneration.

What sea creature is this,

napping in a sleeping bag?

This is a Parrotfish.

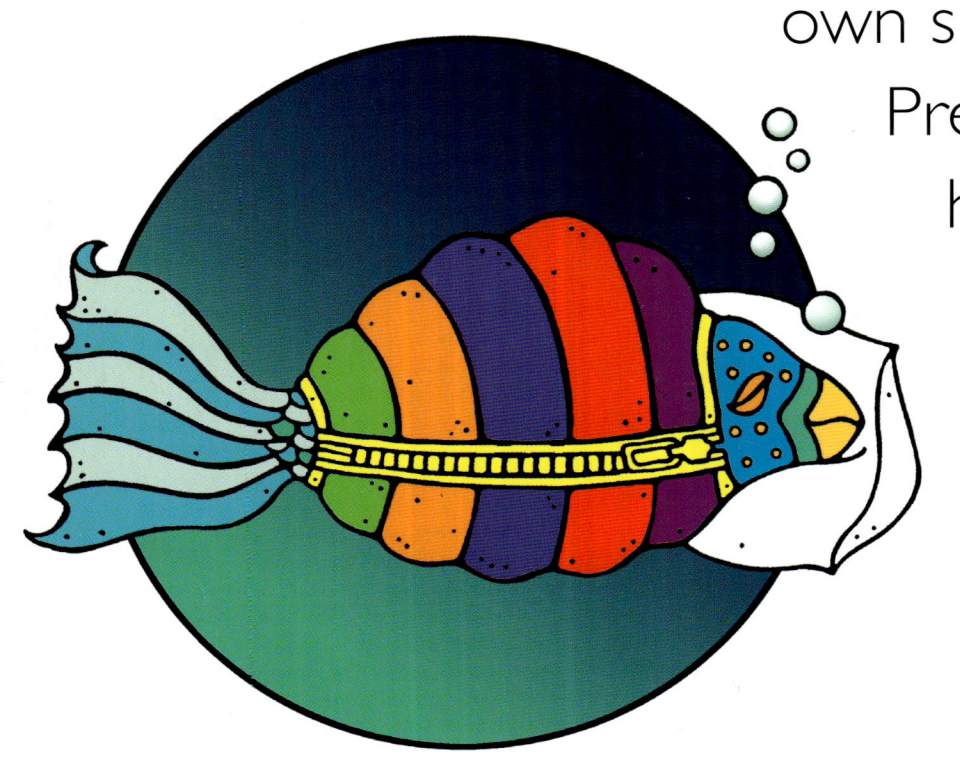

This fish grows up to four feet long and makes its own sleeping bag—of slime. Predators, such as eels, hunt using their sense of smell. Parrotfish are safe inside slimy sleeping bags that block their odor.

What sea creature is this, tying itself in a knot?

This is a Yellow-bellied Sea Snake.

Algae and barnacles sometimes attach to the snake. Like a circus act, the yellow-bellied sea snake ties its three-foot-long body in a knot and moves the knot from head to tail. The running knot sheds the algae and barnacles attached to the snake's skin.

What sea creature is this,

with fangs for teeth?

This is a Fangtooth Fish.

The fangtooth is as scary looking as a movie monster. It even has the nickname, "ogrefish." The sharp teeth, called fangs, are large for this small, six-inch-long fish. The fangs are handy for snapping up a lunch of tiny fish, shrimp or squid.

What sea creature is this,

sleeping with one eye shut?

This is a Dolphin.

Like people, dolphins are *mammals* — they need to stick their heads out of the water to breathe. Whatever you do, don't call a dolphin a *fish*.

But dolphins don't sleep the way people do. They sleep in short naps when half of the brain rests. The closed eye is on the side of the brain that is resting. The other half of the brain is wide-awake and the other eye is wide open. These uneasy sleepers grow from six to thirteen feet long.

What sea creature is this, sailing in its house?

This is a Chambered Nautilus, a sea snail.

These creatures spend their lives inside an eight-inch spiral shell with different rooms or chambers. The nautilus lives in the last and largest chamber. The other chambers contain gas that helps keep the snail sailing along. Fossils of the nautilus show that it lived in the sea while dinosaurs roamed the earth.

What sea creature is this, flying over the water?

This is a Flying Fish.

These fish, about twelve to eighteen inches long, build up speed underwater with their fins close to their bodies. When they leap out of the water they spread their side fins like wings.

Up-up-up they leap four—five—six feet high. What a way to escape sailfish and marlins!

What sea creature is this, standing on stilts?

This is a Tripod Fish.

The tripod fish has three thin, stiff fins that are used as legs. The tripod fish looks like it is on stilts, or like a camera ready to take an underwater photo. The tripod stands, still as a yardstick and just as tall, on the sea floor waiting for passing prey. As small crustaceans swim by and bump into its fins, the tripod fish captures them — to eat!

What sea creature is this,

with no head, no arms, no legs, no brain and no blood?

This is a Sponge.

The sponge is an animal but it doesn't move around like most sea creatures. When a sponge is young, it attaches to a rock or a coral reef or some other hard surface. When water flows through the sponges, they feed on tiny sea animals, called plankton. Tube and vase sponges are small but the barrel sponge is large enough for a person to climb inside.

What sea creature is this, playing music?

This is a Spiny Lobster.

When a lobster drags its antenna across the bumps near its eyes, it makes a sound the same way a bow does moving across violin strings. The noise sounds like a wet thumb rubbing a balloon. The music is not for dancing. It's to keep predators from attacking. The spiny lobster is about as long as a violin bow, almost three feet.

The sea is bursting with life.

Each year, more sea creatures are discovered in the deep, inky waters. The bipedal octopus is a new find. This creature, with a head the size of a walnut and eight long arms, has a tricky way to escape predators. It lifts six of its arms and walks backward across the sea floor on the other two. It can even change shape to look like a coconut as it rolls along.

Much of the sea has not been explored. With each new animal discovered,

we can ask...

What sea creature is this?